PUFFIN BOOKS

Jim Hedgehog and the Lonesome Tower

Jim Hedgehog likes his music loud and heavy – groups like Giant Squid, Spacewind and Crashing Boars. When Jim and his mother go to the street market he heads straight for the music stall to ask for the latest in heavy metal. Jim's mum, who likes a gentler kind of music, buys him a recorder. Back home, they discover to their amazement that Jim's new cassette and the piece in the recorder song book have the same name: 'Lonesome Tower'. After a music lesson with Mum, Jim sets out on an afternoon walk. Little does he know that the tune is leading him to a haunted castle ... with a lonesome tower ...

The musical plot of Russell Hoban's story is particularly original and witty. It should delight all those who are already fans of Jim Hedgehog – and create many more.

Russell Hoban, born in 1925 in Lansdale, Pennsylvania, has lived in London since 1969. He is an internationally acclaimed children's author and has written fifty-eight books for children, including the Frances stories, *Jim Hedgehog's Supernatural Christmas* and the children's classic, *The Mouse and His Child*. He is also the author of six distinguished adult novels, *Riddley Walker* among them.

Also by Russell Hoban

DINNER AT ALBERTA'S
JIM HEDGEHOG'S SUPERNATURAL CHRISTMAS
THE MARZIPAN PIG
THE MOUSE AND HIS CHILD

Jim Hedgehog and the Lonesome Tower

Russell Hoban

Illustrated by John Rogan

PUFFIN BOOKS

PUFFIN BOOKS

Published by the Penguin Group
Penguin Books Ltd, 27 Wrights Lane, London W8 5TZ, England
Penguin Books USA Inc., 375 Hudson Street, New York, New York 10014, USA
Penguin Books Australia Ltd, Ringwood, Victoria, Australia
Penguin Books Canada Ltd, 10 Alcorn Avenue, Toronto, Ontario, Canada M4V 3B2
Penguin Books (NZ) Ltd, 182–190 Wairau Road, Auckland 10, New Zealand

Penguin Books Ltd, Registered Offices: Harmondsworth, Middlesex, England

First published by Hamish Hamilton Ltd 1990
Published in Puffin Books 1992
10 9 8 7 6 5 4 3

Filmset in Monophoto Baskerville

Printed in England by Clays Ltd, St Ives plc

1
Strange Music

Jim Hedgehog liked his music
loud and he liked it heavy. He
listened to Giant Squid and
Crashing Boars and Really
Disgusting Things from the Deep
Swamp. He listened to Truly
Rotten and Monstrous Midnight
and Gravedigger's Express.
He listened to Antimatter and
Beyond the Galaxy and
Spacewind and Black Hole.

He was always on the lookout
for new heavy metal groups.
One Saturday Jim went with

6

his mother to the market. All up
and down the street were stalls
that sold fruit, vegetables, shirts,

trousers, jackets, jumble, shoelaces, batteries, records, cassettes, umbrellas, Elastoplasts, and many other things.

While Mum was buying vegetables Jim went to the music stall. There was a stoat wearing dark glasses minding it. "Strange is my name and music's my game," he said. "If you don't see what you want, ask for it."

"Got any new heavy metal?" said Jim.

"Try this on your earholes," said Mr Strange. He handed Jim a cassette with a handwritten label:

"Is Lonesome Tower the album or the group?" said Jim.

"It's part of a building," said Mr Strange.

"What's the group?" said Jim.

"It's a thing," said Mr Strange.

"Why doesn't it say Itsa Thing on the cassette?" said Jim.

"Cheap cassette," said Mr Strange.

Jim listened to the beginning
of the tape. It sounded like a
hundred tomcats and a thousand
bees in the middle of a hurricane.
"That's not bad," he said.

"Hear any words?" said Mr Strange.

"Sure," said Jim. "Haven't you?"

"No, I haven't," said Mr Strange. "What do you hear?"

Jim sang:

"Crying in the sunshine,
crying in the rain,
trying for what went away
and won't come back again."

"Was that last one crying or trying?" said Mr Strange.

"Trying," said Jim.

"What do you think went away and won't come back again?" said Mr Strange.

"I don't know," said Jim. "Do you?"

"No," said Mr Strange, "I don't. If you like that cassette you can have it for ten p."

"Why so cheap?" said Jim.

"I like to move things along,"
said Mr Strange. He reached into
the clutter at the back of the stall
and took out a recorder. "Here's
a nice little instrument," he said.

Just then Mum turned up.
"Fancy taking up the recorder?"
she said to Jim.

"No," said Jim.

"You can have it for two pound fifty," said Mr Strange to Mum, "and I'll throw in a book as well. He'll be playing tunes in a matter of hours."

"How many?" said Mum.

"Hours or tunes?" said Mr
Strange.

"Tunes," said Mum.

"One at least," said Mr
Strange.

Mum opened the book, *Strange
Pieces for Beginners*. "There's only
one piece in here," she said.

"I'll cross out the s," said Mr Strange.

Mum paid Mr Strange. "We can start this afternoon," she said to Jim.

"I have a lot of prep," said Jim.

"We'll find the time somehow," said Mum.

"Nobody ever got famous playing a recorder," said Jim.

"Nobody ever got deaf from it either," said Mum.

2
Green Bananas,
Fat Alligators

When they got home Mum opened *Strange Pieces for Beginners*.

"See," she said, "it's got diagrams and everything." She showed Jim how to go up and down the scale. "Now," she said, "we'll try this strange piece. It's called 'Lonesome Tower'."

"That's the same title as my cassette," said Jim.

"Different music, though," said Mum. "First let's sing it together. It's only got one verse."

They sang:

"Something pacing on the tower
through the weary darkness long,
hour after lonely hour,
always seems to get it wrong."

"Odd song," said Jim.

"Yes," said Mum, "and it's odd that you were singing *after* me. Haven't they taught you to read music at school?"

"I must have been out sick that day," said Jim.

"I'll teach you now," said Mum.

"Harry Slime is lead guitarist

for Giant Squid," said Jim, "and he can't read music."

"Maybe he's an orphan but you've got me," said Mum. "From the bottom, the lines of the music stave are E, G, B, D, F: 'Eating

Green Bananas Doesn't Fatten'."

"I'd have thought it would,"
said Jim.

"Those are just words to help

you remember the letters," said
Mum. "The spaces between the
lines, reading up from the bottom,
are F, A, C, E, G: 'Fat Alligators
Cautiously Eat Grapefruit.' This
song is in the minor key of . . .''
She pointed to the G line. "What?"

"Grapefruit," said Jim.

"G is right," said Mum. "So where's do?"

"There isn't any dough in grapefruit," said Jim.

"Don't try to be clever," said Mum. "Do is the first note of the

scale and it's on the G line where
I'm pointing. How do we
remember the lines?"

"Five Dozen Bellringers
Gathering Eels," said Jim.

"You're doing it from the top down," said Mum.

"I'd rather start at the top than the bottom," said Jim.

"Do is on the G line," said Mum, "so the other notes go up the scale from there: do, re, mi, fa, so, la, ti do."

"Do, re, mi, fa, so, la, ti, do," said Jim.

"So fa, so good," said Mum.

3
To the Haunted Castle

After the lesson Jim went for a walk beside a stream. He was thinking about "Lonesome Tower" and he was just about to play it when the recorder jumped out of his hands and threw itself into the water.

"I didn't think my playing was that bad," said Jim. As the recorder went downstream with

the current he ran along the bank after it. He was hoping that it would come to a place where he could grab it without getting too wet. But the recorder kept to the middle of the stream, the stream ran deep and fast, and Jim ran with it mile after mile.

It seemed to Jim that he'd left home only a little while ago but already the sun was setting. The countryside around him had changed. He saw half-timbered cottages with thatched roofs and in the distance a castle high up on a mountain.

The evening mists were rising and an owl hooted. At a bend in the stream where the current was

slow the recorder drifted in to the
bank. Jim picked it up and shook
the water out of it.

Nearby he saw the lights of an

inn, The Haunted Castle, and he
heard voices and the clink of
glasses.

When Jim opened the door the
talking stopped and everyone
turned to look at him. The

innkeeper was a stoat wearing
glasses.

"Mr Strange!" said Jim. "What
are you doing here?"

"I live here," said Mr Strange. "Learned that tune yet?"

"Yes," said Jim.

"Good," said Mr Strange. He went outside and closed the wooden shutters on all the windows. Then he closed the door and barred it.

4
Itsa Thing Live

"Why did you do that?" said Jim.

"It gets noisy around here," said Mr Strange.

"You mean frogs and crickets, that kind of thing?" said Jim.

"No," said Mr Strange. "I mean . . ." Just then there came a noise like five thousand tomcats and ten thousand bees in the middle of two or three hurricanes. It shook the inn and rattled the

windows and all the glasses on the bar. Mr Strange covered his ears and crept under a table. So did everyone else but Jim.

"THAT'S ITSA THING LIVE," said Jim. He had to shout so that Mr Strange could hear him. "THEY REALLY SOUND GOOD."

"IT ISN'T THEY, IT'S IT," said Mr Strange. "IT'S THE THING THAT WALKS THE CASTLE TOWER."

"WHAT KIND OF A THING?" said Jim.

"NOBODY'S EVER GOT PAST THE NOISE TO FIND OUT," said Mr Strange.

"I CAN HEAR WORDS," said Jim:

"HOLLERING AT MIDNIGHT, HOLLERING AT NOON, HOLLER ALL THE HOUSES DOWN IF I DON'T FIND IT SOON."

"WHAT'S IT TRYING TO
FIND?"

"NOBODY KNOWS," said
Mr Strange. "TRY PLAYING

**YOUR RECORDER AND
SEE IF ANYTHING
HAPPENS."**

Jim played "Lonesome Tower"
and everything went quiet.

"Maybe it wants help," he said.
"I'm going up there."

"Be careful," said Mr Strange.

"Maybe you'd like to come
with me," said Jim.

"You're the one who hears the words," said Mr Strange. "You'll do better alone."

"Here I go then," said Jim, and
off he went into the night.

In the moonlight Jim could
clearly see the castle standing

dark and lonely on the mountain. In the silence he felt something holding its breath and waiting for him.

Jim found the path and started the climb to the castle. His footsteps and his breathing sounded very loud to him, and the stones loosened by his feet seemed to crash and thunder as they went rolling down the mountain behind him. He heard the hooting of an owl and the squeaking of bats.

There were no lights at all in the castle, it looked empty and deserted. The drawbridge was down, he crossed it. The portcullis was up, he passed

under it. The great door stood
open, inside were cobwebs and
dust.

The moonlight through the
windows made silvery shapes on
the floor of the empty hall. Jim

made his way to the door of the tower, then up the winding stairs. When he stopped to listen there was only silence.

When Jim was near the top of the stairs he thought he heard something sniffling. What if it's something huge and really dreadful? he thought. All I can do is roll up in a ball and make myself as spiky as possible.

Jim came out into the open at the top of the tower. In the bright moonlight he saw something by the parapet. It wasn't very big.

"Who are you?" said the thing.

"Jim Hedgehog," said Jim. "Who are you?"

"Itsa Thing," said the thing.
"*What* are you?" said Jim.
"I'm a girl thing," said Itsa.

"I mean what kind of thing,"
said Jim. "What do you do?"
    "I'm a tower-walking thing,"

said Itsa. "Lots of castles have them."

"I think your 'Lonesome Tower' is a terrific sound," said Jim.

"I don't know what you mean," said Itsa.

"'Crying in the sunshine,'" said Jim, "'crying in the rain, trying for what went away and won't come back again.'"

"Oh, that," said Itsa. "I must have sounded really awful making all that noise but when I get upset I can't help it."

"Why were you upset?" said Jim.

"Walking towers is dead boring unless you have a little song to sing," said Itsa, "and it's got to be exactly right for the particular size and shape of the tower. I'd been working on a song for years and I finally had just the thing for this tower. Then it dropped right out of my mind and I haven't been able to remember it since. I keep trying but I never get it right."

"Why didn't you write it down?" said Jim.

"It didn't have any words," said Itsa.

"But didn't you write down the notes?" said Jim.

"What do you mean, 'write down the notes'?" said Itsa.

"I'll show you," said Jim. He found a pencil stub and a scrap of paper in his pocket and he drew a stave. "First you have to know where the green bananas and the alligators go. Or it could just as well be Eighty Grunting Bears Doing Fireworks or Fish And Chips Eaten Greedily, if you see what I mean."

"Did you say grunting bears?" said Itsa.

"Yes," said Jim. "Why?"

"Bears like honey," said Itsa.
"Honey's made by bees. Bees get
nectar from flowers. My little
song is coming back to me, I was
thinking of bees and flowers when
I made up the tune. It goes like
this," and she hummed it.

Quickly Jim wrote down the
notes of Itsa's song, then he
showed her how to do it. "Now
you'll never lose it again," he
said.

"This time I'll put words to it,"
said Itsa. She sang:

"Sweet as nectar from the
    flowers,
music makes for happy hours –
in my songs will always be
notes Jim Hedgehog brought
    to me."

"That's very nice," said Jim.
"You don't like it," said Itsa,
"I can tell."
"I like it," said Jim. "I guess
I'm just used to your heavy metal
sound."

"You mean like this?" said Itsa, and her voice came out like five thousand tomcats and ten thousand bees and two or three hurricanes:

"SWEET AS NECTAR FROM THE FLOWERS, ROCK AND ROLL THE HAPPY HOURS –

**IN MY SONGS WILL
ALWAYS BE
NOTES JIM HEDGEHOG
BROUGHT TO ME."**

"Wonderful," said Jim.

"But I won't sing like that all the time," said Itsa, "only for you."

"Maybe you can visit my school for the Summer Festival," said Jim.

Itsa did, and she was a big success. Windows shattered for miles around.

Also in Young Puffin

Hairy and Slug

Margaret Joy

Hairy and Slug are quite a team!

TV-mad Hairy, the Mablesdens' large,
brown shaggy dog, and Slug, the family's
incredibly ramshackle little white car,
have the most amazing adventures!
It's surprising how ordinary everyday
outings turn into something quite
different when Hairy and Slug are
around!